For Daddy, Charlie and Jake
Kiss each other for me
— Roralla

To Mum and Nick
with much love — A.B.

Text copyright © 1997 by Rory S. Lerman
Illustrations copyright © 1997 by Alison Bartlett

First American Edition 1997 published by Orchard Books
First published in Great Britain in 1997 by Macmillan Children's Books

Orchard Books
95 Madison Avenue
New York, NY 10016

Manufactured in Great Britain by
BPC Books Ltd
A member of
The British Printing Company Ltd

1 3 5 7 9 10 8 6 4 2

Library of Congress Cataloging-in-Publication Data
Lerman, Rory S.
Charlie's checklist / story by Rory S. Lerman;
pictures by Alison Bartlett. — 1st American ed.
p. cm.
"First published in Great Britain in 1997
by Macmillan Children's Books" — Copyr. p.
Summary: A dog thinks he wants to leave the farm for the
big city, but he finds out happiness is right next door.
ISBN 0-531-30001-3
[1. Dogs — Fiction.] I. Bartlett, Alison, ill. II. Title.
PZ7.L5585Ch 1997 [Fic] — dc20 96-28383

Charlie's Checklist

Story by Rory S. Lerman
Pictures by Alison Bartlett

Orchard Books • New York

Charlie was born in the countryside, but he had his heart set on living in a big city.

When he was old enough to use the telephone and write with a black pen, he sent an ad to a London newspaper.

The ad ran in the personal column.

SIX-WEEK-OLD PUPPY
young, naïve,
and irresistible,
looking for suitably
enthusiastic owner.

Must be under
twelve and
wear glasses.

Applicants please send
photo and references.

Charlie sat and waited for replies. He was the smallest puppy in the litter and the last one out. All of his brothers and sisters had found owners already, and he was feeling lonely.

He spent his days making daisy chains
and sleepless nights counting sheep.
But the sheep always fell asleep before
Charlie did while he was counting them.
Boy, oh boy, he was ready for a change.

Then one day the envelopes started arriving.
Small ones, long ones, thick ones, round ones!
He had a stack of envelopes so high he
needed a trampoline to reach the letters at
the top. He had so many replies to his ad that
he had to hire an assistant to help him sort
through the pile.

MAYBE'S

NO'S

He chose Chester from
the farm next door. Chester
had sneaked into the barn the night that Charlie
was born. He had been his friend ever since and
was eager to help out in any way he could.

Between the two of them they organized two
piles of letters — No's and Maybe's.

Charlie had a checklist of strict criteria.
   "What is criteria?" asked Chester.
   "A list of Must Have's and Must Be's," said Charlie.
   "What about this one?" asked Chester.

I'm Lou. I already have two dogs, two hamsters, two rabbits, one kitten, and four fish. I want you, too....

Charlie shook his head.
   "Must have room for me."

Hi.
My interests are
butterflies and beetles
(I collect them in jars).
I wear thick glasses and
I have big feet for
stamping on ants.

Charlie shook
his head.
"Must be kind
to animals."

I'm Roger. I want to be
in the circus. I need a
partner to join me on my
travels. How about it?

Charlie shook his head.
"Must provide me with a stable home."
"You *are* hard to please," said Chester.

Charlie felt the search would go on forever.
At night he and Chester counted the stars
as they sat on top of the barn. They would
laugh about the letters they had read that
day and sometimes they would play cards
until the birds woke up singing.

"You won't see many stars in London," said
Chester.

"Stars don't matter very much in big cities,"
said Charlie. "There are so many other more
exciting things to look at there — cars and trucks
and tall buildings and lots of different people."

"Oh," said Chester. "I suppose you're right. . . ."

Finally, after two weeks, Charlie opened up the letter of his dreams.

Hi. My name is Naomi. I live on the fifteenth floor in a penthouse suite.

I would love to look after you. I know we'll be the best of friends. I'll take you to all the museums and to the theater. I'll give you eggnog at Christmas and brush your coat till it shines. Be mine....

Charlie ran circles inside
the barn after he read the letter.
Then he ran outside and ran all around
the barn and into the woods and around
the trees. He was so excited!

Chester giggled when Charlie came back: he was covered in leaves and panting.

"Isn't she perfect?" cried Charlie.

Chester looked a little sad. "Yeah, Charlie. She seems great. So I guess you'll be leaving soon."

"Leaving?" said Charlie. "Oh, so I will. I'll need to pack immediately. Will you help me, Chester?"

Chester agreed and walked back home to find a suitcase. Charlie couldn't understand why Chester was dragging his feet.

Finally, thought Charlie, I'll have someone who wants me all to themselves. Someone who will love me forever. . . .

He decided to check through his list of criteria one more time before he called Naomi. He pulled out his page of Must Have's and Must Be's.

Must have room for me.

Charlie looked all around the barn and out into the woods beyond. He could see forever.

Must be kind to animals.

Charlie remembered the time Chester pulled a stinging nettle from his nose. He had put a big pink Band-Aid on it and special first-aid cream.

Must provide me with a stable home.

Chester walked back into the barn then. He was carrying a suitcase and a pack of cards. "I thought you could take these with you," he said. "Maybe you and Naomi could stay up late some nights and play."

Charlie now knew why Chester was dragging his feet. His tail dropped between his legs and he felt very silly, having overlooked his best friend of all.

"I've been thinking," said Charlie. "I'm not so sure dogs are allowed into museums or theaters in London. And I've heard that eggnog can really upset a dog's tummy...."

Chester's face turned all at once into one huge smile.

"Let's keep looking through the envelopes then," he said.

Sunset that evening found Chester and Charlie on top of the barn. They were not sorting through envelopes. They were playing cards and starting to count the stars as they appeared in the sky.

The envelopes kept coming for Charlie. So many that they filled up the whole barn and Charlie had to move in with Chester. Every day Charlie's checklist grew longer and longer.

Must wear red and white striped overalls.
Must be four feet three inches tall.
Must like playing ball.
Must have five freckles on each cheek.

Chester lost track of Charlie's checklist,
but Charlie never lost track of Chester.